KU-798-649

For James and Robert: thank you for lending me your brilliant nicknames, Dodge and Berto – JD

Text copyright © Jan Dean 2001
Illustrations copyright © Chris Molan 2001

Published in Great Britain in 2001
by Hodder Wayland, an imprint of
Hodder Children's Books

A catalogue record for this book is available from
the British Library.

ISBN: 0 7502 3268 4

Printed in Hong Kong by Wing King Tong

Hodder Children's Books
A division of Hodder Headline Limited
338 Euston Road, London NW1 3BH

JAN DEAN

The Haunted Mine

Illustrated by Chris Molan

HODDER
Wayland

an imprint of Hodder Children's Books

Chapter One

"See you soon," said Dad. "Look after Gran!" Then he wound up the car window and drove away down the bumpy track. Mum was in hospital, so Dodge and Berto were staying with Gran for the holidays.

"Come on," Gran said, once Dad was gone. "Take Hoover for a walk while I make supper. And be careful on the hill. Don't fall down any holes!"

"As if," Dodge laughed. "Come on, Berto, let's go."

Hoover bounced around the two boys like a hairy yo-yo as they set off up Fordington Hill. In a couple of minutes they were high enough to be able to see Gran's house below them.

It was an old stone cottage and the roof
dipped as if a giant had sat on it. Fordington
was in the Black Country – an area once
famous for its coal mines – and the hill
was riddled with tunnels. The old mine ran
through the hill the way holes run through
cheese. In some places tunnels had collapsed
and then the land at the top slid down.

Years ago, the land under Gran's house
had slipped and the house sank in the
middle. Builders had made it safe, but the
roof still dipped, and now everyone called
it Crooked House.

"Beat you to the top!" Dodge shouted.

"Not fair!" Berto yelled. "You've got a head start!"

Five minutes later he collapsed in a heap by his brother. Hoover jumped all over him, then sat on his chest panting happily.

"Get off, you great hairy elephant!" Berto groaned.

"Let's go down the other side," Dodge said, and hurtled down the slope.

Dodge didn't stop until he stood outside the old mine entrance. It had closed years ago, but the coal sheds were still there. The tunnel entrance – now blocked off with iron bars – was a black hole in the hill, and the hill was like a huge hump-backed whale. Going inside the dark mouth would have felt like being swallowed by the whale. It was easy to see why the old-time miners had nicknamed the mine Old Jonah.

Berto and Hoover arrived, both panting.

"*Ssh!*" Dodge ordered.

"Pardon me for breathing," Berto gasped. "If I could breathe, that is..."

Dodge gave him a look. "Quiet. Listen."

They stood by the tunnel mouth staring through the bars into the darkness. From deep underground came an echoing moan.

10

Chapter Two

"Weird," Berto muttered. "What is it?"

"I don't know. Listen harder."

The moaning swelled then faded, like the sound in a seashell.

Berto shivered. "Come on," he began, "let's—"

From behind them came a strange, hollow clanging.

Dodge spun round towards the sound. A sudden wind blew past the old coal sheds, whooping through the rusty iron roofs. "It's only the sheds," he said.

Berto smiled. "Spooky..." Then his smile froze. "What's that?" A misty shape flickered then was gone. "There!"

The moaning from the pit grew louder.
Then smoke began to coil up from the
ground. It rose in thick twists and swirled
into six smoky figures. Men made of smoke!
Hoover whimpered.

"Come on, Berto," Dodge said urgently.
"Time we were out of here."

Dodge's heart hammered like a road drill as they ran back up the hill.

"What was it?" Berto asked when he could breathe enough to speak.

Dodge shook his head. "Maybe nothing..."

"*Nothing*?" Berto's voice looped in disbelief. "So we just set the world record for running up Fordington Hill for *nothing*?"

"It was the wind – it spooked us."

"We saw *ghosts!*"

"No. There was smoke, that's all."

"Smoke with arms and legs," Berto insisted.

Dodge looked back down the hill towards Old Jonah. Everything was still and peaceful. Everything was absolutely normal.

"Be sensible, Berto. There's no such thing as ghosts. It was the wind. The moaning, the clanging – then that mist. It was all just stuff blowing in the wind."

"Yeah," Berto said frostily. "Whatever."

"And don't say anything to Gran. Understand?"

"Why not?"

"Because she'll worry about us. And she might tell Dad – then he'll worry. And if it gets back to Mum..."

Berto got the point. Mum had to use all her energy for getting better. She couldn't afford to waste any of it on worrying about them.

"OK," he agreed. "I won't say anything, but that doesn't mean I believe in all this *wind* rubbish."

Dodge sighed uneasily. "What if I find a way of asking Gran about it?"

"Oh, you mean like: 'Gran, tell us about the smoke ghosts we saw round Old Jonah?'" Berto said sarcastically.

"You're really feeling helpful, aren't you?" said Dodge, gritting his teeth.

"Well, how are we supposed to ask about *ghosts* without setting off alarm bells in Gran's head?"

"Leave it to me," Dodge said. "I'll sort it. Now, let's get back for supper."

Chapter Three

"Spaghetti – great!" Berto said.

"Cheese?" Gran asked.

"Is it that stuff that smells like old socks?"

"'Fraid so..." said Gran.

"Great," Berto smiled. "I love that stuff."

Gran laughed. "You are seriously strange," she said.

"Weird," Dodge agreed. Then he had
a brainwave. "So weird that he's decided
to do some extra work for school."

"He has?" Gran's eyebrows rose in shock.

Berto mumbled angrily through his
spaghetti.

"Chill, Berto," Dodge said calmly.
"I'm talking about your history project."

Berto looked puzzled. He wasn't doing
a history project. He waved a twisted forkful
of spaghetti at his brother and gave him
a suspicious look.

"What are you on about?"

Dodge looked him straight in the eye. "You know," he said, slowly and clearly. "*The one about Old Jonah.*"

Berto got the message. "Oh yeah," he said. "*That* project."

Gran glanced from Berto to Dodge. She had the feeling they were up to something, but she couldn't work out what.

"So is there anything you can tell him?" Dodge went on.

"About mining?" Gran asked.

"Not exactly," Dodge explained. "He needs stories about Old Jonah. Exciting stuff."

"There's plenty of that," Gran said. "Mining's dangerous. There are explosions... fires..."

"And smoke," Berto muttered.

Gran stared at Berto in surprise. "You know about that, then?"

Dodge gave Berto a *you're-dead* look, but Gran didn't notice. She was gazing into empty space, remembering.

"The Fordington Smoke used to be quite famous," she went on. "Only it doesn't happen any more. It's a long time since I even thought about it. Fancy you knowing about it!"

"Well, we don't *know*," Dodge said hastily. "Not the *full* story."

Gran smiled. "Right. Let's do this properly. Dodge, shut the curtains. Berto, turn off the lamp. If I'm going to tell a ghost story, I'll tell it by candlelight."

In the candle-glow, Gran began...

"There have been mines in Fordington for two hundred years. The coal here is close to the surface. They didn't have to sink deep shafts. They just cut into the side of the hills then tunnelled to the coal. But the earth has secrets. Faults in the rock make tunnels collapse. Underground springs wash away pit props. Sometimes men were crushed by rock falls, sometimes they were buried alive. Imagine those poor souls trapped in the hill, moaning in the dark tunnels, locked in the darkness for all time."

"Spooky," Berto whispered.

"Terrible," Gran said. "One day gas
exploded and the mine caught fire. Thirty
men were lost. The village blamed the pit
boss. He should have sent a fire-man in
to check for gas.

"That night the villagers marched to
Old Jonah. The boss was there, in charge
of the men putting out the fire. The villagers
were angry. They carried flaming torches
and they banged on cans and buckets...

"They demanded to see the boss. He said it was an accident. Not his fault. 'May I burn in hell if I'm to blame,' he said.

"Then it happened. All around him, thick, choking smoke rose from the earth. People say it was the ghosts of the dead miners, come for their revenge... Everyone ran.

"Next morning they found the pit boss lying on the hill – stone-cold dead."

Chapter Four

"Ghost smoke," Berto whispered.

"I hate to ruin a good story," Gran sighed.
"But there is an explanation."

"What?" asked Dodge.

"I told you – the coal is close to the
surface here."

"So?"

"So, when the fire started it set the coal
alight. And the smoke from it rose through
the soil and came out of the hill."

"Just ordinary smoke then?" Dodge said
"Like from any old fire?"

" 'Fraid so," said Gran. "Nothing spooky about it."

"But what about the dead boss?" Berto asked.

"I get it!" Dodge said. "The villagers blamed the boss for the deaths in the mine. They hated him. In the confusion and panic when the smoke came, any one of them could have killed him."

"I reckon that's it," Gran agreed. "Now – sorry, boys, but you can't put it off any longer. *Bedtime*."

After lights out, Berto stared through the darkness towards Dodge's bed.

"What if the smoke *was* ghosts?" he whispered.

Dodge sighed. "Gran explained. It was just plain fire smoke from the explosion."

"What about the smoke we saw?" Berto insisted. "Old Jonah's been shut for forty years. There've been no fires, no explosions."

"Drop it, Berto!" Dodge snapped. "I'm supposed to look after you. I promised Mum. She'd go mad if she knew I was letting you go on about all this ghost rubbish. It'll give you nightmares. Now shut up and go to sleep."

Chapter Five

Life at Gran's settled into a routine. Most
evenings Dodge walked Hoover on the hill,
but then the spell of good weather ended.

"Walking tonight?" Gran asked anxiously.
"In this rain?"

"It's easing off," Dodge said. "Besides,
Hoover needs a run."

Dodge put on his cagoule and climbed the hill. Below him was Old Jonah. In the distance he could see the red brick houses of Fordington. Then a movement in the grass caught his eye. Smoke!

Dodge gazed at the coiling smoke rising in a snaky line. It gathered itself into distinct shapes – six smoke-men. Their eyes glowed like blue flames – staring straight at him!

"*Hoover!*" Dodge shouted. "Here, boy!" Then he turned and ran.

Half-way down the other side of the hill, Dodge looked back. On the crest of the hill a blue light flickered. A line of ghostly shapes looked down at him. Then lightning cracked the sky and suddenly the rain was a downpour. It blotted out the sinister figures on the hilltop, but Dodge's heart still pounded at his ribs.

They've found me, he thought. *They've left Old Jonah and tracked me down!*

Chapter Six

When Dodge arrived back at Crooked House his face was white and he was shivering. Gran took one look at him and sent him for a hot bath. Berto itched to know the full story, but there was no chance to talk until bedtime.

"That smoke we saw... I saw it again,"
Dodge began. Then he told Berto how the
smoke ghosts had loomed above him, how
they had stared down at him as he ran.

"Ghosts..." Berto whispered. "I *knew* it!"

"But they followed me," Dodge said.
"They came after me... Why?" He listened
to the rain pelting the window, like a
hundred bony fingers drumming on the
glass. "They're out there, Berto," he
whispered. "And they know where we live."

It rained and blew all week, so hard that Gran banned Dodge's walks. Dodge was glad. The hill was no longer a great place to be. Now it was full of menace.

Then, on Friday, Dad rang. "The good news is: Mum's doing well. She'll be home in a few days. But the bad news is: there are floods on the Fordington road. I can't get to see you tonight."

"But you've *got* to come—" Dodge blurted.

"I can't," Dad said helplessly. "No one can. The police have closed the road."

Later that evening the lights flickered then went out. The TV died.

"The storms have damaged the power lines," Gran said. "We'll have to light some candles and—"

Suddenly the room began to shake. The dishes on the dresser rattled then crashed and smashed on the floor. Outside a huge roaring rumble echoed across the hill.

Gran took a torch and went outside. She came back wet and windswept. "The rain's washed rocks down the hill," she said. "The track to Fordington's blocked."

"Then we're cut off," Dodge said.
"Trapped."

"Look!" Berto pointed to the window.
Thick white smoke was seeping in, dropping
over the sill like a smoke waterfall.

"I don't know what that is," said Gran
hurriedly, "but I think we'd better get out
of here right now."

Chapter Seven

Gran and the boys grabbed their coats and wellies and headed out into the storm. The rain fell in solid sheets. Gran took the flashlight and led the way.

"It's OK – there's an old footpath. It'll be terribly overgrown – no one uses it these days."

She turned towards the path, but instantly, out of the ground in front of her a wall of smoke fountained up.

"The Fordington Smoke!" Gran said, dismayed. "If the underground coal is burning there could be cave-ins on the hill."

"This way!" Dodge shouted. But no matter which way they turned the smoke blocked them. And from the smoke shapes formed. Spectres in the smoke – their eyes flickering like blue lightning.

Desperately Dodge swung his torch beam across the ghostly smoke. There was a gap!

"Run for it!" he yelled and darted through.

Then they heard a powerful gushing sound.

"What's that?" Berto shouted.

"Water under the hill," Gran said. "The rains have flooded the old tunnels. If they collapse there'll be a landslide. We must get out of here!"

But more smoke spectres sprang up in front of them. Shooting from the ground, one after another, rows and rows of them, barring their path.

"We'll have to go across the fields!" Dodge shouted.

"Too dangerous," Gran shouted. "That way's full of old land-slips. It's unstable!"

She turned back towards the footpath but the ghosts rose up. They were all around, pushing, shoving, herding them over the field like sheep.

"Get away from me!" Dodge yelled, but the smoke just thickened, clotting the air around him. Ghostly eyes glittered everywhere. Dodge shuddered as a thick coil of smoke wound round him. "No! *No!*" he screamed.

Chapter Eight

The ghosts towered above Dodge to form a smoky wall. Like a giant wave breaking, it fell on him and he felt that he was drowning in a sea of smoke. Then everything changed – it was like a dream. Soft voices spoke to him, gently whispering: "*Trust. You must trust. We will keep you safe. Too many died in Old Jonah. Too many. Now we are the guardians. Follow. This way. This way. Safe. S...a...f...e.*"

The ghostly voices faded, but Dodge understood.

"Follow the smoke!" he shouted. "It's on our side!" He grabbed Berto and set off across the field.

"Not that way!" Gran yelled, but Dodge took no notice. She had no choice but to follow him.

As they reached the outskirts of the village they met the rescue party.

"Thank goodness you didn't come down the old footpath," the police sergeant said. "There was a mudslide. If you'd come that way—"

"We'd have been squished," said Berto.

"I reckon you would," the sergeant said.

"Will Crooked House be OK?" Berto asked.

"It's survived worse," Gran said. "We'll fix it."

Dodge stared up at the hilltop. Through the darkness and the rain a faint blue glow flickered.

"Thank you," he whispered.

Across the hill a low wind moaned and a wisp of grey smoke floated above it, a ghostly hand waving goodbye.

DARE TO BE SCARED!

Are you brave enough to try more titles in the Tremors series? They're guaranteed to chill your spine...

Deadly Dodgem by Anthony Masters
Jack never loses his temper... that is, until he sits in car Number Six at his parents' dodgem track. Then he's dangerous. Deadly. What is it about that car? Could Number Six have a dark secret?

The Headmaster's Ghost by Sam Godwin
Danny's school trip would be great if he wasn't being bullied by Adam and Melissa. They try to scare him senseless with stories of the evil headmaster's ghost who is said to haunt the building. Then one dark night, Danny accepts Adam's dare to prove that he's not scared, but it brings more than he bargained for...

The Empty Grave by Rebecca Lisle
When Jay visits her cousin at Gulliver House, strange things start to happen. Who is the mysterious child that cries in the night? And what is behind the sealed door? Jay and Freddie must discover the truth before it's too late...

All these books and many more can be purchased from your local bookseller. For more information about Tremors, write to: The Sales Department, Hodder Children's Books, A division of Hodder Headline Ltd, 338 Euston Road, London NW1 3BH.